A SOUL FOR HIS SOULMATE

BEYOND FRIENDSHIP...

ARUL SANTHOSH D

ISBN 979-888503757-0

To my soul mates and to my wife.

Contents

Acknowledgements

I wish to convey my gratitude for each and every reader who supports and encourages my writings continuously. My special thanks for my better half who is sharing the life with me in all my ups and downs and to my lovable kids who keep me in joy and make my life more beautiful. When it comes to get feedback of my writings, my wife is the one who is always my first reader of my books and gives her suggestions and continues to be the first reader for this book as well. My sincere and heart-felt thanks to Mrs. Margret Alphonse for doing editing work and valuable suggestions for my work and make this book a complete one. And finally, I deliver my thanks to my blossom pals who cheer with me and back me up in my downfalls and for their love shown to me.

This book is all about the bonding of friendship and the life of a young man, who ripens the fruits for seeding the honesty, keeping patience and having trust in his life that matches this quote: 'Seed good things and ripens the good of everything'. The characters in this story are unreal and the story is purely written in imagination.

Prologue

In every man's life there will be the thirst of quenching his dreams. For most of them, that becomes the turning point to excel and even to fall. Here was a man, named David who was 22 years old, hunting and yearning for his dreams. He was an ordinary person who finished his higher studies with the help of his God father and seeking for an opportunity to survive in his life. He was grown up in an orphanage since his childhood. He lost his parents at the age of three in an accident and he had been adopted by the orphanage and there, he grew up and became a man.

He decided to leave from that orphanage to start a new life of his own. He started to work in a branded car showroom as a sales consultant. He resided in a mansion for monthly rent. Two years had gone and his life became like a pendulum which started its oscillation here and there. That oscillation could not make him free and had not kept him in the state of rest.

Many a few questions were provoking in his mind. He was busy in finding the riddle of his life. He led his life in solitude after coming out from the orphanage. The main thought process for him was to get a partner for sharing his feelings and everything he had to that person.

David went to church and attended the holy mass every day. At the chill weather in a winter season, at early in the morning, after the holy mass got over in the church he just walked alone in the road and his mind occupied by many questions to get solution. He had seated on a stone bench at the roadside. As he was sitting and beholding the vehicles on the road, he saw a young woman came for walking along with a dog. His eyesight started focus on the young woman and the dog she took with her for walking. Within few minutes, they had been hidden behind the long truck which was parked at the road side. The snow partially covered the road and the beam of the Sun light penetrated the snow. As the breeze gently pushed the snow away, the woman and the dog were being seen in his visual frame when they had passed the truck. She had been captivating his soul and dropping an L-bomb on him. She crossed the stone bench and went ahead. His eyesight slowly turned left and focused her. He got up from the bench and followed behind her.

After walking for a kilometer the young woman entered her house. He was getting worried as his happiness ended in one kilometer. He crossed her house and walked few meter away from her house, there he found a grocery shop, at the nearby distance. He went to that shop and asked for water bottle to drink. He came out and opened up the bottle and started to quench his thirst underneath a roadside tree. A minute later, he noticed that girl who arrived to grocery shop. She looked at him from the corner of her eyes and entered into the grocery shop. Her eyesight made him something to his inner-self. It pulled and stole his soul, he felt. He drank quickly and threw the bottle in the garbage can at the roadside and got ready to follow her.

She came out of the shop and started walking to her house as he too began to follow her behind. She suddenly turned back and made him fear.

"Who are you? And why are you following me?" she asked him.

"I am not following you. I came here to the shop to get a water bottle and I just have my walking in the morning time." He said.

She stared at him and turned back towards her house. She was standing at the gate and her eyes were staring at him till he crossed her house. He crossed her house and continued to walk with a disappointment that the happiness he had been lost within a few minutes.

The next morning also David seated on the stone bench at the same time after the mass ended. She stared at him again while returning to her house after finishing her walking along with the dog. He did not follow her. After she entered her house, he went to that grocery shop and bought some snacks as he was expecting her presence for the grocery shop. But she did not come. He continued this routine action as his regular practice for a week at specified time, he did it regularly.

A week had gone and on Sunday morning 6'clock mass, she entered the church for attending the holy mass. To his surprise he saw her entering the church to attend the holy mass as every Christian had attended the holy mass on Sundays.

She was surprised to see him in the choir that he was playing keyboard 'cling...cling' sweet notes from the keyboard. She used to attend evening mass on Sundays. From that week onwards she came for morning mass. She was shocked by his presence in the church at the morning mass.

David had stopped his routine action which he followed on the previous week. Pretending as if he did not notice her, David went back to his room after the mass. At every week Sunday mass only, she could see him while he was playing the keyboard.

CHAPTER ONE

BROKEN THE MELANCHOLIC SHELL

Three months had gone. He had not visited and seen her in the early morning in between, other than the Sunday mass in every week at church.

One day she was waiting for the bus or other transport at the bus stop in the remote area which was 30 km away from the city limit on the Trichy- Madurai highways. David was returning to office after finishing the test drive for his customer. On his way, he saw that girl, standing at the bus stop. He stopped the car there and he got down from the car.

“What happened? Why are you standing here?” He asked her.

“I am waiting for the bus to return from here.” She glanced at him head to foot, with a haste look on both sides of the road and said.

“Come I will drop you at the city. Let into the car,” he said, with an intention to help.

Hesitating to go with him, yet she got into the car. He closed the window glasses, switched on the air-conditioner and played the melodious song mildly. The song lyrics went on this way...

"poonkatrile unswasathai thaneyaga thedi parthen! Kadal mel oru thuli vilunthathe athai thedi thedi parthen!"

This is one of the familiar love-feeling songs in Tamil.

"Hai, I am David." He gave his intro to her.

"I am Helen." She said and glanced outside through the window randomly and her lips started humming the song.

"Are you a college student?" he asked.

"She gave a quick answer, "No, I am a teacher in a private Matriculation school."

"I thought you are a college student," he said. And he did shoot another question, "What is your major?"

"I am a B.Sc., Maths teacher with B.Ed.," she replied.

The car entered the city limit and reached the bus stand. He unlocked the door and she got down from the car.

She made her head down and looked through the door window and said, "Thank you so much."

"The pleasure is mine." He bowed to her.

In the evening, the phone rang. Helen picked up the call.

"Hello" she said.

"Helen! This is Ramya from Coimbatore."

"Hey Ramya! How are you? What a surprise call from you after a very long time. Wait, wait..." She pinched herself and said.

"I am fine dear." Ramya said and asked her, "How about you?"

"I am in pink of health, Ramya. What's the news?" Helen asked with enthusiasm.

"Can you do a favour for me? Ramya requested her.

"What can I do dear? It's my pleasure." replied Helen.

"I need a video of inter university music competition. Do you have it?" Ramya asked her.

"Let me check and get back to you, dear." The call went on for fifteen minutes talking about their college PSG.

She was searching for the CD in her book shelf where she kept everything in it. Finally she had found it.

She inserted into the player disc and played the CD to check and confirm the video whether it was the one she was looking for. She saw the background screen at the stage decorating beautifully with some colourful arts and also it was written with words as 'Inter-University Fine Arts Competition 2000-01'. Whole watching it for few minutes, she heard an announcement from the MC desk mentioning the participant name David, to perform at the stage. To her surprise, she saw the musician David, who played keyboard in the church every Sunday. David with Guitar instrument gave a solo performance, made the auditorium with a pin-drop silence. He drew all of their attractions with his singing and playing simultaneously. Helen was impressed in his melody from his vocal and in the instrument he played. Before that she has seen him singing and playing the keyboard, the devotional songs. First time, she heard the movie song with a Guitar.

Helen copied the video on her laptop and took extra copy of it for her friend Ramya.

The next morning, David was seen seated on the stone bench once the mass got over. Helen along with her dog saw him sitting on the stone bench with the corner of her eyes and crossed him. After taking few steps, she turned back to know what he was doing. David noticed her that she had noticed back and looked at him. He stood up and started to walk behind her with 50 meter distance. She once and again turned back and had a casual glance at him and she expected him to come closer to her. With little hesitation and fear, he crossed her and went ahead.

Suddenly her voice reached his ears.

"David," she called him by his name. He was shocked.

"Did you call me?" He asked her with slight hesitation and more eagerly.

"Yes"

She added, "I saw the CD, about your performance at an inter-University music competition held four years before at my college."

"Oh! In which college?" he asked her in soft voice.

"PSG College," she said.

"You played the Guitar so well and impressed me." She complimented him.

"Thanks for your compliment, Helen" he smiled.

"Which is your native place?" He asked her.

"Trichy, here only" she added, "I went to Coimbatore for my studies. I did my schooling and my B.Sc Mathematics at PSG College."

He asked "Did you stay in hostel?"

"No. I stayed in my uncle's house there."

"Bye! See you later, David", she said and went into her house.

Next day morning again he saw her while sitting on the bench with the same environment. She saw him and waved her hands. She came to the spot.

"Good morning Helen!"

Glancing at him, she said, "Fine morning, David."

"Yesterday I saw you sitting on the bench. You are here today also... Why?" She asked.

"Just wish to free my mind from loneliness, Helen." His voice revealed the feel of solitude.

"Oh! Are you alone? She asked him.

"Yes, I am living in the mansion."

"Your parents?" enquired her.

"Gone...up above the Heaven I was brought up in an orphanage from my childhood." He said and added, "When I was three years old my parents died in an accident. Hence then, I had been living my life there only. After finishing my studies I left the orphanage and began my new life."

"Sorry, I should have not asked you about that." She said in compassion.

"What's wrong in it? It's all the will of God. It's 'my fate' Helen."

With an intention of getting her number, he said, "Here is my card. I am a sales consultant. If you need any assistance please feel free to call me."

"Sure David." She conveyed.

A call came from her at 4'clock in the same evening.

"David, this is Helen" She said.

"Pleasure to hear from you, Helen," he was surprised.

"Are you free now?"

"Why Helen?"

"I am going for shopping around 4:30PM. Will you accompany me?" She again asked.

He saw his watch and conveyed, "Oh! Yes Helen. I am always free at your service."

"Where are you now?"

"Now I am in my house. I am getting ready for shopping. Within ten minutes I will come out of the house." She said.

She wished to get his suggestion and asked him, "Where shall I come?"

"Let us meet at Iyankar Bakery in Chathiram. See you there soon."

"OK fine." She said and switched off the mobile.

He started his bike and rode to Chathiram Bus Stand. He reached the spot at 4:25PM. She has not come, sat at the table and waited... She entered the bakery and sat opposite to him exactly at 4:30.

"How was the day? Ordering two plates of Samosa, he queried her.

"Good. And for you?" she asked him in return.

"It started good and hope it will end up better or the best."

"Is it not a working day, today?" He threw a question to her.

She said, "Today is Saturday, half working day only."

"Oh! You are lucky. But I have six full working days in a week. Only Tuesday I am having my week off. Even Sunday, I have to work." He said with a bit of frustration.

The Samosa arrived at the table and both started to bite.

"Hot Samosa, delicious to eat," David said.

"Then, at what time do you go to church to attend the Sunday mass?" She threw a question.

"I usually attend 6AM mass." He said.

"I know David." She said.

Raising his eyebrows he uttered, "How?"

"I see you at 6'clock mass every Sunday. You are the one playing key board in the choir." She told him.

"Yes, I play keyboard in the morning mass every day." He added, "I too have seen you many times on Sundays."

"Every day?" she shot a question with an intention to confirm.

"It is my regular practice and in fact my passion. And I love to play it for God every day." He conveyed and drank the glass of water.

"Great! David." She complimented and kept the plates aside after finishing it.

"How did you learn to play the instruments?" she enquired with eagerness.

"I learnt it from the church father. He taught me in the orphanage." He told her and he continued, "Later with self interest I learnt to play all the instruments. Especially Keyboard and Guitar are my favourites."

"Wow! David, you are gifted." She exclaimed and praised him.

They paid the bill and winded up from there. They went for shopping together until 8. After finishing her shopping, he dropped her in her house and he had returned to his mansion.

CHAPTER TWO

SORROWFUL SOUL

Many days after, he felt happy and got relaxed that he could have killed the loneliness from him. The happiness continued for a year. Often Helen met him and talked to him. He felt that the queen and his angel arrived to show him the paradise world, where he was being drizzled in delight and sunk into the ocean of ecstasy.

It was on Feb 14th, every couple was celebrating the lover's day. They shared many gifts with each other as their token of love. Many made their proposal to their loved one as they finally revealed the sweet pain, which was stocked in their hearts. Here too, one heart released his joyful and sweet pain in his heart to his beloved.

David dialed Helen's landline and after the third ring, she picked up his call.

"Hello" said Helen.

"Helen, this is David. Shall I meet you today evening at 'Coffee Day' shop?" David requested her.

She thought for few seconds and finally said, "Yes." And she threw back a question to him, "How much time does it take?"

"Just less than half-an-hour I suppose." He said to her.

"Okay then we will meet at 5 PM." She conveyed and fixed the timing.

"Fine," he told and the call ended.

The moment he kept the receiver on the phone, his heart beats pumped up fast and he felt a bit of fear and hesitation in him. His mind was thinking of what would happen once he said it. He was restless. The evening came and he waited for her in Coffee Day shop for her arrival. The clock almost hit 'five'. She came and seated opposite to him in a private cabin.

"Good evening David" she greeted.

"Fine eventide" he too greeted back.

"How is your work David?" she asked.

"It's going on fine as usual. How about you, Helen?" he asked the same to her.

"It is fine." She told him. And she placed a card on the table.

"What's it?" he raised his eyebrows.

"Invitation"

"Invitation! For what" he raised the question.

"School Annual Day, the day after tomorrow"

"Oh! Fine," taking deep breath he said and continued, "Helen, I wish to share an important thing with you," his voice had somewhat broken as he was in fear and restlessness.

"What David? Anything good news do you carry?" she asked him with smile.

He conveyed to her, "About my life in future."

"What is it?" Her eagerness was shown in her eyes.

"In my life, I travelled mostly in the path of darkness which was more painful and loneliness. I fought against those and struggled to lead the life as normal." He started narrating his feelings.

And he added, "I am blessed with an angel who lightens my life colourful and bright. Yes, I mean to say 'YOU'. You are the core cause for the changes made in me. You have shown me the seventh heaven. You are my angel, ruling MY HEART AND SOUL seeding the hope in me and making my solitude disappear.... Will you be my sweet heart forever in my life? Will you be the queen for this king?" He proposed his love to her.

Helen was in complete silence for few minutes and said, "I have lot of respect for you, David. I understand your feelings, but I am sorry David. I am not able to accept your proposal. I have spent beautiful, golden moments with you. It was memorable and cherished. I am impressed by your music and fondness you have shown to me. My father has already chosen a life partner for me. I won't be against his decision. I like to fulfill always his will and wishes. Our engagement is going to be soon."

But he saw her lovable eyes that conveyed him something different. He had fallen into the beautiful and graceful sights of his angel.

Dead silence prevailed there for more than two minutes and David said to her, shaking his shoulders "It's my wish to be with you. So don't feel for it. And thanks for the wonderful memories you have given me."

"Come, let's move." He paid the bill and they both left the shop with heavy heart.

David went to his mansion with great disappointment but he did not react much. He concentrated on his work to get more prospectus customers to get on the business during day time. At night, he tried hard to come out of his loneliness, because his dreams and wishes had broken. The musical instruments healed him as he played the tunes of what his soul had sung.

He could not forget the moments with her and it flashed his mind often. He was once again arrested by the melancholy. He needed the change in his life style to comeback into normal. Two months gone by and David shifted his residence to Chennai as he got transfer there in the same franchise with a promotion. Before he went to Chennai, David met Helen and gave his Chennai address where he had been accommodated.

"Helen, I am going to Chennai on transfer tonight. Here is my address." David extended his card to her and added, "Please send letter and keep in touch with me. I expect your call and letter at any time."

"Sure! Take care, David. I will send my wedding invitation soon."

David returned back to his room and did pack all his clothes and musical instruments. The Sun had set and soon he departed from the mansion, booked for a cab and waited.

The cab arrived and he got into it. As the journey started, he rewound his pleasant memories with her in Trichy. The days with Helen were the sweetest in his life. Definitely he was going to miss her the days to come. Her eyes often sparkled his mind and senses, which was his inspiration, pleasure and everything. Five hours had passed and the cab reached Chennai at 3' clock at night. He was dropped in the place where he got accommodation. He settled in his room and had a nap for four hours.

The next morning, he joined the duty in his new office. He focused more on his job to avoid the lonely feelings. He worked hard and got the good prospectus for his business. He impressed his boss by his nature of work. Soon, within the short span of six months, he was promoted as a team leader from senior sales consultant. And simultaneously, he attended some auditions for music.

A year later, he got a post from his angel, Helen. He opened it and saw an invitation card, a letter and a photo attached with the letter. Seeing the photo, he was surprised. He had seen Helen and his God father, Antony who was the sponsor for his studies when he was in the orphanage. He too saw the engagement & wedding invitation. He opened the letter and started to read.

A LETTER FROM AN ANGEL

Hai David,

I hope you are fine with the blessings of God and from the prayers of mine. How is your new job at Chennai? My engagement is on coming Sunday. And the wedding is on the first week of next month. I have attached my invitation card and a photo of mine with my father. Kindly, please do come for both the occasions. David, I have a guilty feeling that I hurt you when you approached and proposed me. I feel sorry for it. I cannot disobey my father as he is a so kind and gentleman. I lost my mother in my early days where I was six months old. My father asked her elder sister, Sarah to take care of me. After that I had grown up at my aunt's house along with their daughter, Gracy in Coimbatore. Monthly once or twice my father came and saw me in Coimbatore. I did my schooling and college studies there only. My father remained single and did some services for the society. He is a business man and he is a familiar man in the society. He is so generous and kind to all. He is the person who always keeps his promise. Once he gives assurance to someone, he won't get it back. He keeps his words to be true in his action. That's why I told you like that on the other day. Please forgive me if I had hurt you. I feel very guilty to face you in person. My father was asked by his friend that he wanted to get alliance for his son with me. My father and my aunt accepted his wish and will. I do not know what to do. I leave it to God to do something for me. Please take care of you, David. I am expecting your presence on the occasions. Please drop me a reply. Take care.

Yours sincerely,

Helen Antony.

CHAPTER THREE

THE SACRIFICE

The week-end came; David applied for four days leave prior, for the next week. On Saturday night, he started his travel to attend his angel's engagement. He felt the storm and thunder smashing his soul and his dreams at the same time. But he hid his pain and went to see Helen on the occasion. On Sunday morning, he arrived to the wedding hall where the engagement was to be held. He saw his God father, Antony at the entrance receiving the guest with a board smile.

Seeing him, "Hai David, my son! How are you?" Antony enquired.

"I am fine God father with your blessings." He said.

"Come and meet me in my office tomorrow. I wish to talk to you." Antony said to him and gave him his visiting card.

David was in some confusion and fear of why his God father asked to meet him and finally with low voice he responded him, "Sure God father."

"Please go inside and take your seat, my son," he told him by tapping his shoulders gently.

He had his seat in Orchestra wing, where the troop asked him to join them for singing. Within few minutes, his angel arrived on the stage with a gorgeous appearance.

She was pretty in that attire. She was like a lily covered with rose petals and jasmine. Her face was pale and sick as she lost the charm that her eyes could reveal it; yet she contended to be normal. Her eyes glanced randomly and it was hunting for someone in the crowd. She heard the voice from the Orchestra wing that the person she was looking for. David had sung a song in the orchestra band. His voice was so sweet and pleasant to hear. He sang a beautiful melodious song and impressed everyone gathered there. Helen saw him singing first time in person. The tears almost dropped from her pretty eyes and she managed to wipe with her kerchief. With the wishes from their relations and friends, the engagement ring was exchanged by the new couple as they are going to marry soon. The kith and kin of the couple and their friends conveyed their wishes to them. David too conveyed his wishes. The function ended with the grand party. The next day, David went to meet his God father, Antony in his office as he was asked to come.

"Welcome David, my son! Please be seated." Antony gave a warm welcome to him.

"Thanks" he said and seated politely opposite to him.

"Do you know why I asked you to come here, my son?" Antony threw a question.

"No," he said in a low voice.

"I wish to tell you an important thing which I kept within me for years." Antony told him by looking at his friend's photo frame in the table.

"What's the thing God father?" he asked politely.

"David! I have decided that it is time for you to know about yourself." He said to David.

And he showed a photo to him and continued, "He is your father. You are my friend's son. Your father and I are close friends and business partners too. Your father is a sole owner for the property what I am maintaining now. I am just a working partner with him. Unfortunately in a car accident, your parents died. Your mother Victoria died on the spot and your father was taken to the hospital and was getting treatment for his life. As he was in the conscious stage, he had given me the power for his properties and asked to run the business as my own and take care of you too. Within two days, he passed away as the treatment did not give his life back."

David with his eyes full of tears, asked "What are you saying God father?"

"Yes my son David. But I did not know what to do at that time. I had to take care of you as well as the business. So I approached the orphanage where you were grown up. They had taken care of you. I concentrated on business. I am thankful to the orphanage to make you a perfect man. Even if you grew with my care, I could not have made you like this, my son. They only shaped you as a man what you are now."

Antony had a deep breath and added, "Within a year, my wife Clara became sick and passed away, leaving my child and me in sadness. I was very much depressed by the death of your father and my wife. I handed over my daughter's future to my sister and asked her to take care of my daughter in her town itself. My daughter was grown up under the care of my sister and you were grown up under the care of that orphanage. I started to focus on the business to fulfill my friend's ambition and his dreams.

"What is my father's dream God father?" David asked him to know about it.

"At the early stage, your father had gotten a franchise for bicycle. He asked me to be a managing partner for his franchise. We struggled at the beginning but we never gave up the challenges. We made it control of our business and got success after many failures. Then he took a branded car franchise, and that also become a successful one. Our business was going on a good pace, and then came the disaster that your father passed away. I was completely depressed after losing your father and my wife within a short span of time. The fate had played in our life and gave an incurable wound to us. I do not know what sin that my daughter, you and I have done to suffer for life long," his eyes filled with tears and he wiped off with his fingers.

"Your father often conveyed to me that we wanted to open at least four branches for our franchise in the main cities. We had opened one in Trichy. We had to open in Chennai, Madurai and Coimbatore. It was his wish and vision and he was moving forward to attain his dream. Unfortunately, he was no more. I have been running alone in the race for years to fulfill his desire." Antony said to David.

"I am thankful for you God father for sacrificing all your life to fulfill my father's dream." David said to him with tears.

"His dream is not yet fulfilled. We need to open two more showrooms, one at Madurai and another at Coimbatore. The remaining task should be done by you only, my son. I will guide and support you in all aspects. So only I asked you to work here itself, in our show room after your studies got over. And I also sent you to Chennai to get exposure of the business. I hope, you gained plenty of experience in these years while working. Here after, you are the sole proprietor, I will transfer the power and the properties in your name. These are your father's properties and they belong to you only. I have my own, in my sources of income. Within two days, we will finish up the formalities legally. Please make sure your presence here, for another couple of days." God father conveyed him.

"You are really a God father to me. I do not know how to convey my gratitude to you for making my father's dream alive and fruitful for the years." David got some emotion and hugged his God father.

Two days later and the legal procedures got over and David took charge as the Head of his father's business. He had planned to reside in Trichy for ten days and spent twenty days at Chennai in a month as he took charge of both the branches.

His God father had spent one week with him to guide and get him know everything about the business and the administration. David quickly learnt all things related to his business from his God father. He started to execute the things and monitored the two branches closely under his control.

"You are like your father when it comes to business, my son. I am seeing your father in you. You are very sharp and keen to learn and execute the things like your father." His God father praised him for his skills he got naturally.

"It is from you only my God father." David gave the whole credits to him in return.

Two weeks had gone. Antony's friend came and met him. They both discussed and planned about their children's marriage.

"After marriage, you no need to get worry about the business, my friend. My son, Edward will take care of Chennai branch and you take care of Trichy. Why are you hurting your health with the travelling? Be relaxed, and take care of your health." Antony's friend, Joseph said to Antony.

"My dear friend, I knew it already about my health condition because of the restless travelling. So I decided and handed over the business to the owner's son. Now I am totally free and relaxed." Antony told his friend.

"What are you saying Antony?" Joseph threw a question to him with confusion. And he enquired, "Who is the owner and his son?" He wanted to know it.

"Be calm, my friend. I am a managing director only for the franchise. The owner is my close friend, James who had passed away twenty-five years ago. He gave me the power to run the business and now, his son takes charge of the franchise. I transferred the power and the documents in his name and handed over everything to him legally." Antony told him.

"I have spoken alliance with your daughter for my son only because of the franchise branch in Chennai. I thought, you will hand over the Chennai branch to my son after the marriage; but you are saying like this. I don't know what you will do. I need the branch in Chennai to be registered in my son's name." Joseph ordered him with a high pitch tone.

"I am very sorry, my friend. I will not do wrong to my friend, James and to his son. I will not do anything against my inner self." Antony made his decision clear to his friend, Joseph.

"Then let us drop the marriage that is going to take place next week." Joseph conveyed him with the great range and angry and went away from that place.

Antony was getting into depression after Joseph winded up from his house. His health condition also did not support him to keep his body normal. His thought was full of his daughter's future. He dialed to his family doctor and asked to attend him immediately. The doctor arrived within ten minutes. Antony was restless and worried about the life of his daughter. The doctor checked him and called for the ambulance service to admit him in the hospital. He was admitted in the hospital for treatment. Helen and David were informed about it. They rushed to the hospital to see him. Antony was kept in the ICU. The doctor called Helen and David and explained them about his health condition.

"He had a mild heart-attack and as of now, we have given first-aid to him. We examined and found out two critical blocks in the blood vessel at pulmonary vein during the angio. The blocks need to be removed. He needs a by-pass surgery." The chief doctor conveyed them.

"Please go ahead for it doctor," David said to the doctor and saw Helen for getting confirmation and she nodded with worried eyes.

The team of heart surgeons made surgery for Helen's father. David and Helen were waiting outside the operation theatre. Five and half hours later, the chief surgeon came out and informed them.

"The surgery was over. He is being monitored closely, as he is in observation. He will be getting normal within few days. We have removed the blocks. He will be shifted to the normal ward tomorrow evening." The chief surgeon seeded the hope for them.

"Thank you very much doctor," David conveyed his gratitude to the chief doctor.

"Please don't give him any pressure hereafter. His health condition will be critical again and it hurts him in all the ways." He advised and took leave from them.

CHAPTER FOUR

HARDEST TEMPEST

Joseph and his son Edward did not even come for formal sake and see Helen's father. They had just a business deal in the name of marriage, where Helen was kept as a prey in it. They had trapped many people and made them as prey for their desire of wealth. On which, Antony was one among them. Luckily, Antony and his daughter would have escaped from their trap.

One week later, Antony got discharged from the hospital. He needed to take complete rest in his home. Weekly once he had to take regular health check up. He should also maintain proper diet. David had recruited a nursing staff for his God father to take care of him.

Two months passed; Antony called his daughter to have a chat with her.

"My child, I made a big blunder that I accepted the alliance with him for you. With God's grace, their mask had been torn and I could see their real face. Or else you would have become prey to them." Antony told Helen with a sign of relief.

"Don't feel for it dad. Everything will be done according to the will of God." Helen said, with a relief.

"Yes my child. What wrong had we done to others, to ripe the fruit of evil? We are saved by the God." He told her daughter and getting relaxed.

"We faced many struggles and this is one among those." She conveyed.

"Whatever it is, but you rightly said my child." Antony said and nodded his head for her sayings.

David came to meet his God father, Antony in his home where he saw his daughter Helen also sitting beside him as they were chatting each other.

"Come on my son, how is the work going on?" Antony asked David.

"It runs smooth and how do you feel now God father?" he enquired his health.

"I am feeling better my son as you two children are with me, why should I feel for something?" He said with courage.

"Tonight I am leaving to Chennai. I will be there for couple of weeks. Please take care of you God father. Even when I am in Chennai, my heart and soul will be here only." David said to him as his sight has glanced Helen too.

He could see her eyes longing for something from him when he looked at her.

"Take care of you and take care of the business my son. My blessings will always be with you." His God father blessed him as he gently touched David's head.

David went to Chennai for monitoring the business there. Every evening, he called Helen and asked about her father's health and gave reminder about the check up and medicines with his recorded voice over the phone, even though he was in busy schedule. He attended some important meetings with the clients. He was very busy in work for a week. For a span of week, he could not hear his angel's voice due to the protocols that he had with himself. A week had gone and he could get time for breathing in other activities. He got relaxed. His angel's sight which he had seen one week before was flashed often in his mind. He searched for the letter which she had written for him. He noted the address. In the evening, He dialed the landline number of Helen's house. The ring went on and Helen was anticipating the call from him.

"Hello!" she said with a sweet voice.

"Helen! How are you?" he asked her.

"Oh! It takes one week of time to ask my health." She said to him jovially and kidding.

"No, Helen. Little bit busy in work. So only I could not speak to you freely." He explained to her.

And he questioned her, "To which address shall I send letter for you, Helen?"

"You can send it to house address itself, David. I only receive it from the post man." She told him.

"How is your father?" he asked her.

"Day by day he is feeling better," she said.

"Take care of you, Helen and your father. I will post a letter tomorrow in register post. Please write a reply and give it to me in person when I come there." He conveyed to her.

"Take care, David" she said and the call ended.

He made himself free from the work after the Sun set. He converted his feelings into words as he started to scribble.

A LETTER TO AN ANGEL

How are you Helen? I hope you are in pink of health. Many things happened in my life since I had seen you from the first time to now. All changes occurred because of you and your father only. I am thankful to your father for my life time. His sacrifice for the friendship with my father is immeasurable. He has been living his life for my father's ambition only. I do not know how I am going to show him my gratitude and honour him for his trueness in friendship. He has done so much for me. I wish to fulfill his desire and my father's ambition as well to give it to them as my gratitude. For that I am preparing myself strong both mentally and physically. You are the only source of inspiration to overcome the failures and to face the challenges in the race to get succeed. I have felt the path of heaven in your presence and the torches of hell in your absence. Your captivating sight lights up my life and removes the strain as it showers me the delight with its prettiness. I am very much thankful to you for making my path of life so divine and beautiful as you are my angel gives the hope and happiness for me. I am in need of fulfilling your father's desire. I could not spend much time with you but your thoughts are overwhelming in my mind and soul always, with which I could lead my days. Your sight consoles me whenever I am in depression. It shrinks all the pain and gloom in me. Take care of you and your father. Helen, kindly speak to your father freely, as I could see in your eyes and I could feel the thoughts in you that you have stocked something within you. I will come and see you after ten days.

Yours,

David James.

CHAPTER FIVE

BOOM AND BLOOM

David was in tight schedule in his business protocol. He conducted some client meetings and he also had the staff meetings for his staff. He had offered many surprises to his staff to reduce their financial burdens and made them secured from their insecurities. He had offered free education for the employees' children and he started to deposit two thousand rupee monthly as recruiting deposit for their children other than their salary. Each and every family of his staff was insured as he covered them with family health insurance for two hundred thousand.

The employees were very much in delight and they felt some burdens were reduced from them. All of them gave their best in the work with full potential and strength.

David returned to Trichy to see Antony, his God father at his house after he had spent three weeks in Chennai.

"My son, David welcome young and energetic boy." Antony welcomed him.

"How are you feeling God father?" he asked him.

"I am feeling better my son." He said to David and added, "David, I have heard your announcement for our staff from one of them. I feel very much proud of my son, but how do you manage to do it?" Antony appreciated him and asked about his plan.

"I am not going to do those in the cost which I need to invest for it, but I am going to execute it in our profit itself. I believe it will be successful. You just wait and watch God father how the things will be getting changed after two quarters in this year." He assured his God father about his plan.

Antony praised him, "Great and well done my boy! God blesses you abundantly. I am pleased with you."

As the talk went on, David saw Helen inside the house. She was very pretty and beautiful. She came and seated beside her father.

"How are you David? How is your work?" Helen queried about him and his work.

"I am fine. The work is going on smooth." He responded her.

"Come on my child, you two have a chat. I will take leave from you to my room." Antony said and went to his room.

David saw her pretty eyes that overwhelmed with happiness after seeing him.

"How are you Helen? Did you get my letter?" he asked her.

"I am very much happy to see you David. I am fine. I had read your letter. I miss you very much and I am expecting your presence for these days, finally it comes now." Helen said in a low voice.

"How is the work for you? Have you taken your father for the regular check up?" David asked her and enquired about her father's medical checkup.

"It's fine. Weekly once I take him for regular checkup. His health is getting better day by day." She answered him.

"That sounds good, hearing about his health. And special thanks to you for taking care of him Helen." David complimented her.

"You are the reason for his fast recovery and his joy. You had carried his burden on your shoulders that he had been carrying for years." Helen complimented him this time.

Helen asked his choice of drinks, "What do you drink, coffee or tea David?"

"Let us sip tea, Helen" he gave his choice.

As the talk went on between them with a cup of tea in their hands, killing the tea sip by sip, David was arrested in her two twinkling stars and he was made freeze in her charm. Her sparkling eyes conveyed many things to him that he could sense the depth in it. They had chatted for hours as they were sunk in the ocean of contentment.

"Thanks for this moment to cheer myself with you, Helen." David grasped her hand and smiled.

"You have only brought my smile back. I am very much grateful to you." Helen thanked and handed a letter to him which she had written for him.

David got the letter from her and made his exit from Antony's house. His eyes were filled with hope and he was revamped with new energy from his angel. Helen's eyes were also bloomed with blossom as the Sun had set behind the mountains which covered with snow. They started to feel that their life has just begun. They dreamed about the new beginning of their life as if they had witnessed the happiest world where they would have lived in it. They were ready to enjoy the joy of beauty, quenching the pleasure of wine together, and merging into the blissful ocean.

David after reaching his room made himself refresh and relaxed. He took the letter which had been received from his angel. He started to read the verses of his angel as it showed below.

A LETTER FROM YOUR ANGEL

David, I have to thank you for bringing back my smile to me. I was completely disturbed and worried about my life and also about my father's health. God had heeded my prayers and let me free from it. I read your letter. It made me happy and proud to lift my father's ambition on your shoulders. My prayers and heartfelt wishes are always with you forever, David. My father is happy and satisfied of your work and regains his confident back by the way you take over the business in your own style. He wishes prosperity and success and fulfils his friend's dream. I made you hurt in the past and offended your feelings. I feel sorry for it. Now it is the time for me to show respect for your feelings and accepting it. I am very much previleged to have you in my life. I wish to be your queen, my king. I am able to feel the chillness in my inner self whenever I think of you. I can sense the happiness in me and it reflects in my face that you can see it. Your words console me whenever I got depressed. You have stolen my soul, my thoughts are full of you always. I wish to hold your hands in our journey of life. My eyes are longing for you as if it were a bee which would look for honey on the flowers. I am ready to live my life with you as your queen. I started living with you in my dreams. And I wish this dream happens to be in reality. Will you accept me as your better half and give me a place in your heart, my sweet heart?

The Queen of Yours,

Helen.

CHAPTER SIX

REVAMP AND REJUVENATION

After reading her letter, his happiness went up to the sky as if he flew and touched the deep blue sky with the ecstasy. Within a minute, the phone rang as he picked up the call.

"Hello, David here" said David, with the curiosity to know who had called him.

"I love you, my king. Will you accept me as your queen?" Helen proposed him and gave another surprise with her sweet voice.

"Helen! My queen! You showed me the path of Heaven." David pleased her, with an excitement.

"I love you too, my dear queen!" he added.

"Good night, my dear king. Sweet dreams. I see you in the morning David." Helen greeted.

"Sweet dreams, my queen!" this time said David and the call ended.

With a sense of joy and pleasure, David started to tune the guitar and composed his feelings as music. A few minutes later, phone rang again.

"David here" he picked up the call.

"Sorry to disturb you sir. I am Charles Daniel, your secretary." his Personal secretary called him.

"Yes, Daniel. What's the news?" David enquired politely.

"I have happy news to convey sir. The company is ready to get our proposal of owning the franchise at Coimbatore and Madurai." Daniel gave him the blow of double delight.

"Oh!!! I am being hit by more excitements. Thank God" David conveyed back his happiness.

Daniel added, "You are supposed to attend the meeting in Singapore tomorrow evening with the company senior faculties for delivering our presentation to them. Just now I received a mail from them about this."

"Tomorrow?" asked David.

"Yes sir. You have flight for Singapore at 3 a.m early morning. Now the time is 10:30 p.m sir. Please look on to it sir." His secretary intimated his departure.

"Oh! Have you booked ticket for my journey, Dani?" David asked.

"Yes sir. I have arranged everything for you. And a surprise is awaiting there at Singapore sir." Daniel told his Boss.

"Oh surprise! What is it?" David asked with intention to know.

"I was told not to reveal. You yourself will know it when you get there sir." said Daniel.

"Let me see that there itself. What time I need to be at the airport?" David asked for the timing.

"Be ready at 12 sir. I will come and pick up you in your home." Daniel told his boss.

"That's fine. I will be on time." David said to his secretary and ended the call.

Many things went on in David's mind. He was being showered with sweet moments from the evening. Despite all the things happening around him, he got ready at 11:45 p.m and his secretary had also arrived to pick up him.

They reached the airport on right time and finished their boarding process. The flight took off on right time and they flew to Singapore.

CHAPTER SEVEN

THE PROMISE

The next day was dawn at Singapore for David and his secretary Daniel. They were received great hospitality from the company at the time they landed at Singapore and welcomed them to the hotel where they were accommodated. David got refreshed and got ready to attend the Board meeting on time. Once he reached the meeting hall and to his surprise, he saw his God Father, Antony in the meeting.

"Come on my son, David. It is your day, today. Wish you all the best." Antony made his wishes to him by hugging.

"God Father, you are here" David said with a great shock.

"Yes, my son. I am your managing partner. I suppose to be here and I wish to be with you today." Antony told him.

"My goodness, I am really excited to see you here with me. Thank you so much." David said with cheers.

The board members arrived to the spot and Antony welcomed them with great pleasure and introduced his friend's son David to the board members. The proceedings of the meeting began. David gave his proposal presentation to the members of the board and shared his executed plans to them. Everyone in the board meeting was impressed and his God Father was feeling happy and proud of David, the way he took over the business to this pinnacle. The chief members of the board appreciated David. They delivered their hearty congratulations to both David and Antony for the business. The meeting ended in a great and satisfactory way.

"Well done, my boy! You have made it for your father." Antony hugged David and congratulated him.

"It is purely your effort, God Father. You should deserve this." David gave the full credits to him.

And David asked his God Father with surprise, "How did you come here?"

David's secretary intervened and said, "That's the surprise which I said boss."

"Oh! That's the great and happy surprise for me." David swore to him.

"Come with me, my son. There is another surprise awaiting you." Antony gave another blow of bombshell to him.

Antony took David with him into a party hall. There David could see his queen in gorgeous attire with her Sarah aunty, uncle and Gracy.

"Here is your Queen, my son. Go and hold her hands" said Antony to David.

And Antony added, "I know, my son. My daughter told me everything. And Helen is so privileged to have you as her life partner. Now, the engagement is going to be held for both of you, my children."

David was sunk in the delightful ocean as he was speechless. Helen came closer to David and held his hands and said to him, "Here I am your queen. I wish to walk along with you for the rest of my life. Will you be my king to hold my hands ever?

David printed his warm lips on her forehead and told, "This king's life is handed over to a beautiful queen. I had done something great in this life before to have you as a life partner."

Antony gave the rings to both of them. They exchanged the engagement ring in each other's finger. And within a span of next three weeks their wedding took place in their home town Trichy.

One year had gone; the board members in the company accepted the proposal for getting two franchises in Madurai and Coimbatore and they offered to David a double blow of two more additional franchises at Salem and Erode for his achievements in the past one year.

Another double blow waited for David that Helen had given birth to twin boy babies. David and Helen named their children as 'James' and 'Antony' for the symbol of their fathers' friendship and their true bonding of relationship which they were having in their life.

Dear readers,

Thank you so much for spending your time to read my novel. Kindly give your feedback and comments by dropping an email to my email id: arul8785@gmail.com

9 798885 037570

Printed by Libri Plureos GmbH in Hamburg,
Germany